This book belongs to

....

Tom Mouse And The North Pole Mystery!
is the second book in the series,
The Fantastic Adventures of Tom Mouse.

The first book, **You Can Do It Tom Mouse!**
along with merchandise and resources for
schools can be found at **www.TomMouse.co.uk.**

Inspired by journeys and dreams with Tom Barr

First published in the United Kingdom in 2021

Text copyright © 2021 Dicky Barr

Illustrations copyright © 2021 Joanna Scott

Graphic design by Clive Batkin

978-1-9999569-3-6

Tom Mouse
And The
North Pole Mystery!

by Dicky Barr
& Joanna Scott

Tom Mouse loves his grandad. Grandad Mouse was a great explorer when he was young.

Tom spins his globe, and where it stops is where he will go.

"I am going to travel to the North Pole!", says Tom.

Grandad Mouse reads from his newspaper,

"Young mice write to Santa at The North Pole, but no mouse has ever seen Santa. It is a great mystery!"

Tom Mouse is worried.

"Grandad, do you think I can get to the North Pole *and* find Santa?"

"You can do it Tom Mouse!", says Grandad.

A new adventure to prepare for.
Tom made a long list of all the
things he would need.

Gloves
x 2 pairs

Wellies

Anchor

Flares

Cheese

Big Jacket

Woolly Hat

Thick Trousers

warm socks

Running Shoes

Scarf

Cheese
Biscuits

Ernest Shackleton Bunny

Compass

It would be very cold
travelling across the vast
ocean and at the North Pole.

Disco Ball

~~Goooles~~
~~Gooogles~~
Goggles

Snow Shoes

He wondered what
else he would need.

Rubber Ring

Mobile Phone

Snow Board

The list went on and on...

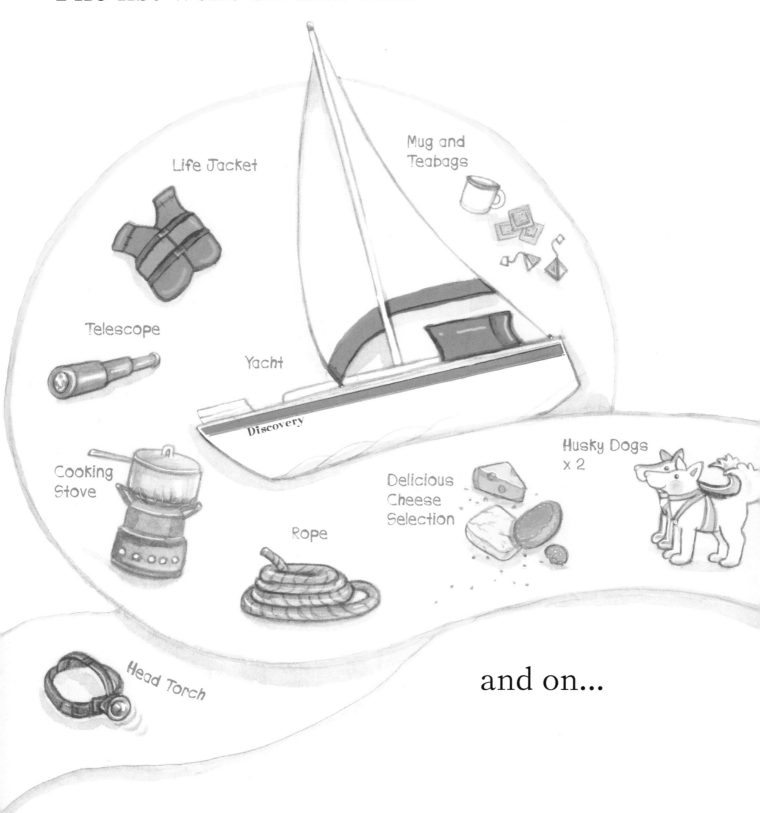

Life Jacket

Mug and Teabags

Telescope

Yacht

Discovery

Cooking Stove

Rope

Delicious Cheese Selection

Husky Dogs x 2

Head Torch

and on...

...and ON!

Until finally it was finished.

So, with help from Grandad Mouse,
and not so much help from the huskies,
Latte and Mocha, Tom was ready to go!

"Good luck! You can do it Tom Mouse!",
says Grandad Mouse.

The wind blows,
and Tom sails away.

It was all going
very well until...

...the wind stopped blowing!

"A sailing boat needs
the wind in its sails",
sighs Tom.

"We are not going to make it", cries Tom.

Then Tom hears

BOOM YA!...

BOOOM YAA!...

BOOOOM YAAA!

and he turns around to see...

"Hi, I'm Alfie, the tenor orca."

"A tenner, that sounds quite cheap!", says Tom.

"I am a tenor singer!", booms Alfie.

"Wow, Alfie, your voice is so loud! How deep can you go?", asks Tom.

"About 1000 metres!", says Alfie. And they all laugh.

"The Mousettes and I will sing you on your way!", says Alfie.

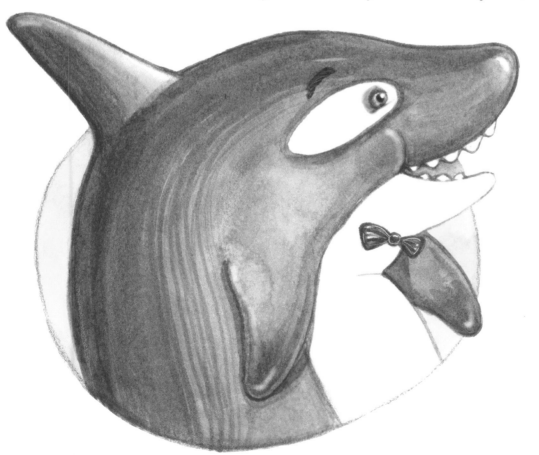

Tom shares cheese and biscuits with all of his new friends.

The Mousettes play beautiful music, and Alfie starts to sing with his powerful voice.

They finally arrive at the Arctic ice, and set off towards the North Pole.

At a very large water filled gap in the ice...
"How are we going to get across?",
says Tom.

Then they hear...

SWOOSH!...

SWOOOSH!...

SWOOOOOSH!

and they turn around to see...

"Hi, I am Leonardo, the artist and engineer.
I will help you across the water."

Leonardo makes a quick calculation,
and taps his computer screen...

SWOOOOSH!

and a beautiful ice bridge is created.

Leonardo - Creator of Global Cool

"Wow, this is wonderful. Thank you Leonardo", says Tom.

Tom shares cheese and
biscuits with Leonardo.

"Are you a civil engineer?", asks Tom.

"Oh yes, I am
very friendly",
says Leonardo.

And they both laugh.

The adventurers carry on their
fantastic journey.

"Goodbye, kind Leonardo", shouts Tom.

"Stay cool Tom Mouse!",
calls Leonardo.

Further on, the snow gets deeper and deeper. It gets colder and colder and the wind gets stronger and stronger...

... it is a

BLIZZARD!

"HEAVE!", cries Tom.

...but they are stuck!

And then Tom thinks of
Grandad Mouse saying,

"YOU CAN DO IT
TOM MOUSE!"

Tom makes one final H-E-A-V-E!
and...

    ...they are free!

A little bit further and Tom
will be at the North Pole...

"I Did It!"

Tom is the first mouse to have travelled to the North Pole!

Tom Mouse is on top of the world!

"Thank you to all my friends!",
shouts Tom.

He thinks about
his Grandad too.

Then the ground starts to...

S – H – A – K – E

And the ice opens up to reveal...

"WOW, IT'S SANTA!",
shouts Tom.

Tom Mouse has solved
the North Pole Mystery!

"Welcome to the North Pole Tom Mouse!",
calls Santa.

"Please come inside my workshop
and I will show you round."

Hundreds of busy elves
are making beautiful toys.

"This is wonderful!",
says Tom.

Santa shows them just some of the amazing presents being made, then he says, "Oh! Look at the time!"

"We must fly, Tom Mouse!"

"We have presents to deliver to all of the young mice around the world!"

Tom Mouse is so happy as
he flies through the night sky.

WHEEEEE! shouts Tom.

...Santa has one more very
special delivery to make...

"I knew you could do it!"
Grandad Mouse is so proud of Tom.

Tom Mouse says,

"Grandad, I wonder where my next fantastic adventure will be?"

How many puffins did you see
in the book?

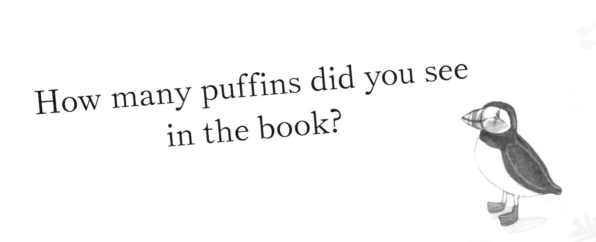